Abundant Love

BY ALBERT HUMPHRIES

DORRANCE
PUBLISHING CO
EST. 1920
PITTSBURGH, PENNSYLVANIA 15238

Dorrance Publishing Co
585 Alpha Drive
Suite 103
Pittsburgh, PA 15238
Visit our website at *www.dorrancebookstore.com*

ISBN: 979-8-88925-991-6
eISBN: 979-8-88925-717-2

Abundant Love

Contents

Introduction

Please allow me to introduce you to Mr. Albert Humphries' *Abundant Love*. His use of everyday situations and down-to-earth writing style appeal to the readers through the language we know as love. We all have a desire for love in common, be it love of God, family, and friends. In this collection of poetry, every installment includes the word "love." The verses speak to the heart of the matter at hand to love and to be loved. From the blinding of the mind to unconditional all-inclusive levels of love. Affection, attention, and acceptance are vital components of this vested interest called love. Mr. Humphries uses common language to convey universal messages of love to capture the reader's attention. This poetry is intended to enlighten, entertain, and encourage the hearers to have faith in themselves, their relationships, and in humankind. The following poems speak to the mind, body, and soul, just like air to breathe, water to drink, and food to eat.

Not only is Mr. Humphries an award-winning published author, but he is also a lover of good music, good food, life with laughter, and a historian. For Mr. Humphries, writing poetry stimulates his creativity and drives his passion to spread joy, laughter, and to make the readers think about their everyday lives and experiences. He is blessed to be a blessing to others, myself included. His poems about love focus on the daily ins and outs of our lives in a way that can be experienced no matter what walk of life we come from. When you crave another person, it is an overwhelming desire just like wanting your favorite dessert. Once you taste it, it's like heaven on earth in your mouth. Just the sight of that sweet treat makes you smile with anticipation and has your mouth watering. The use of sensuous, subtle, and/or simple wording is intended to relate to everyone's sense of worth and desire to love and to be loved. We all can appreciate singing in the rain, or a walk in the park, or dancing in the living room with our sweethearts. Something as delightful as a touch from the right person can spark an avalanche of creativity. For example, the first time a newborn baby grasped your pinky or as inviting as your lover giving you a massage. Mr. Humphries' use of scintillating rhyming and repetition in short-story form expresses perseverance in bad situations as well as satisfaction in good and keeps you intrigued from beginning to end.

I hope you enjoy reading this ongoing body of work, just as I have. Since becoming Mr. Albert Humphries' personal assistant, I have witnessed a light being shone about the commonality of humankind on paper and the complexities as it pertains to interpersonal relationships. I have found myself examining the answers as to why it is so hard for us to tell someone else that we love them and mean it indeed, and not just lip service. The certainty of love being more than simply using terms of endearment. Moreover, I have learned this journey called life is well worth the effort to invest, explore, and experience the possibilities.

– Candace Gamble

Does This Mean I'm in Love?

Albert Humphries

My mere thoughts about you produce goosebumps, whenever you summon, like a puppet, I jump. Yes, you are a vital part of whatever I do, when I think of myself, I think of you. Does this mean I'm in love? Does this mean I'm in love? I feel a fluttering, tingling and tickling sensation inside of me, it must be the flame of my heart burning passionately. Unquestionably, it's no ordinary heartburn, at night in bed it makes me toss and turn. And whenever I do fall asleep, my dreams are pleasant and so sweet. Does this mean I'm in love? Does this mean I'm in love? I distinctly recalled the first time we met, nervously, I broke out in a cold sweat. I tried to make my first impression the best, I had a lot to say, but I remained speechless. Does this mean I'm in love? Does this mean I'm in love?

I Just Love That Girl

Albert Humphries

Man, I met this chick the other day, she knew exactly what to say. She was so proud to mention how quickly she got my attention. Her smooth complexion is pecan tan and her sexy body I just love to scan. I just love that girl! I just love that girl! She's the most sensational girl in the world. Sensational! Sensational! I saw her one night in my dreams, she's the prettiest girl that I've ever seen. I'm so glad she accepted my date because man, she's the perfect mate. She sure does know how to take a hint, man, this girl is very, very intelligent. I just love that girl! I just love that girl! She's the most sensational girl in the world. Sensational! Sensational! She said that she's a one-man girl and only my love makes her head swirl. Her mellow voice is music to my ears, I could listen to her for a million years. She makes me feel like a king, man, this chick just got everything. I just love that girl! I just love that girl! She's the most sensational girl in the world. Sensational! Sensational! Her love could make a blind man see, man, she really put a hurting on me. I'm one very happy and lucky guy, I got a lovely girl money can't buy. I got to hold on to this special chick, without her love, I really would get sick. I just love that girl! I just love that girl! She's the most sensational girl in the world. Sensational! Sensational!

I Love You in My Own Way

Albert Humphries

I love you in my own way, my love is here to stay. I think you are a very sweet girl, sporting your jet-black Jerri Curl. I love you in my own way, my love intensifies day by day. I love your big sparkling eyes, there will never be any good-byes. I love you in my own way, regardless of what others may say. I love touching your soft skin, it excites me, now that's not a sin. I love you in my own way, it's free, you don't have to pay. I love the way you walk, my love is real, not just talk. I love you in my own way, I really hope it's ok. Try your best not to be lazy, being constructive and productive is not crazy. I love you in my own way, like horses and cattle love hay. I'm hypnotized when we make love, only we know and the Lord above. I love you in my own way, there's a time to work and a time to play. I understand your agonies and ecstasies, one day you will fulfill your fantasies. I love you in my own way, you can't mold it like clay. There's one thing you must accept, only you can take the first step. I love you in my own way, tell me what else can I say. Continue to be respectful and nice, nothing beats that at any price. I love you in my own way, it's secure and will not go astray. Don't let the rat race get you down, I love you even when you muscle up a frown.

I'm Hungry for Your Love

Albert Humphries

This here urge, which is called hunger, well, I just can't stand it much longer. I'm hungry, I'm hungry for your love. I'm craving for your steaming emotion. Be aware, I desire more than one portion. I'm starving for your hot affection. It happens to be my favorite selection. Baby, I'm hungry and I hope you are too. I'm hungry for your love and I'm hungry for you. Don't hesitate to give me a lot, I prefer mine piping hot. Yes, I have a mighty big appetite, I'm more than ready tonight. I'm hungry and I hope you are too. I'm hungry for your love and I'm hungry for you. I'm eager to hear your sweet conversation, but I need to ease this uneasy sensation. I appreciate your warm wishes, but right now I need your delicious dishes. Baby, this here urge, which is called hunger, well, I just can't stand it much longer. I'm hungry and I hope you are too. I'm hungry for your love and I'm hungry for you.

I Need Some Loving

Albert Humphries

Baby, love is what I need. Oh, yes, indeed! I need some loving, I need some loving. To get it, I know how. I need some loving and baby, I need it now. I have already cast my bait; I have to sit and wait. For you to sock and knock me out, your love is what I'm talking about. Baby, love is what I need. Oh, yes, indeed! I need some loving, I need some loving. To get it, I know how. I need some loving and baby, I need it now. Like birds need wings to fly, I need your love, that's no lie. I got my facts and act together, a sure way to love you forever. Baby, love is what I need. Oh, yes, indeed! I need some loving, I need some loving. To get it, I know how. I need some loving and baby, I need it now.

Is My Love Strong Enough?

Albert Humphries

To avoid falling into any traps, we can seal and bridge all the gaps. I'm going to give it my best shot to reinforce all the weak spots. Is my love strong enough, strong enough for me to have you? Please tell me the truth, is my love strong enough, strong enough for you? Your true heart is what I must secure and I'm taking some steps to make sure. If you don't have any objections, may I ask you a simple question? Is my love strong enough, strong enough for me to hold you? Please tell me the truth, is my love strong enough, strong enough for you? I hope that we will stick together, a bond that last us forever. You see, I'm dishing out all I got and I still have some serious doubts. Is your love strong enough, strong enough for me to keep you? Please tell me the truth, is my love strong enough, strong enough for you?

Isn't Love Lovely?

Albert Humphries

Isn't love lovely, isn't love lovely? Lovely as love can be, your lovely love got a hold of me. I hope my baby will show up soon, it's such a lovely afternoon. I'm mesmerized when she comes my way, hey baby, you look so lovely today. My body is burning like fire, tuned to satisfy your desires. Isn't love lovely, isn't love lovely? Lovely as love can be, your lovely love got a hold of me. Your lovely love is sweet and nice, your lovely love I wouldn't sacrifice. It's lovely to be in love with you and it's lovely that you love me too. I'm going to love you year after year, my days are special when you are near. Isn't love lovely, isn't love lovely? Lovely as love can be, this is the way the world should be. It's wonderful that I am your man, we will enjoy life together hand in hand. Yes, you are a lovely girl, you and I in this lovely world. Isn't love lovely, isn't love lovely? Lovely as love can be, your lovely love got a hold of me. Your lovely love is as lovely as love can be. Your lovely love got a hold of me. Your lovely love got a hold of me.

Loveache

Albert Humphries

Baby, I got a terrible loveache and your medicine is what I should take. I'm sick of being lonely and sad. Love, your love is what I wish I had. Yes, the suffering is beyond belief. But a shot of your love will bring quick relief. Baby, I got a terrible loveache and your medicine is what I should take. So, please, please don't delay, fill my prescription right away. Affection is what I need the most, come on now, baby, give me a dose. Baby, I got a terrible loveache and your medicine is what I should take. It perks me up when I am feeling down, I'm so fortunate that you are always around. It's important that you are aware, I do appreciate your tender loving care. Baby, I got a terrible loveache and your medicine is what I should take.

Love Abuse

Albert Humphries

Love abuse, love abuse, you made me a victim of love abuse. Love abuse, love abuse, you took total advantage of my weakness. That's the only reason I put up with your mess. At that time, I was lonely and having fits, so I made my love too easy for you to get. But now, I gotta turn you a loose, because you made me a victim of love abuse. Love abuse, love abuse, you know right or wrong, I'll still love you. You must be sick to exploit me the way you do. It doesn't bother you to treat me like dirt, coming from the one I love, it really hurts. But now, I gotta turn you a loose, because you made me a victim of love abuse. Love abuse, love abuse, pains and hardship are definitely the results, stemming from your complaints and insults. You used to be kind, generous and polite. Now, you don't care to do anything right. That's why I gotta turn you a loose, because you made me a victim of love abuse. Love abuse, love abuse.

Love Attack

Albert Humphries

Love attack, love attack, hey, baby; are you aware of the fact, love attack, love attack will put you smack flat on your back? Love attack, love attack, hey, baby; a love war is about to start, I'm going to fight my way into your heart. I got the firepower to do you in, but in this war both sides win. I'm going to make you fight me back, you won't be able to resist my love attack. Love attack, love attack, hey, baby; are you aware of the fact, love attack, love attack will put you smack flat on your back? Love attack, love attack; baby, there's no chance of a ceasefire, winning this war will fulfill my desires. You said that I had to fight for this and then intimidated me with a hot kiss. I'll charge at you with all I got, baby, all I need is one good shot. Love attack, love attack, hey, baby; are you aware of the fact, love attack, love attack will put you smack flat on your back? Love attack, love attack, baby, I'm going to lay a bomb on you! I'll part your heart through and through, I'll use body-to-body combat. You will surrender, because you can't stand that. Baby, I will continue to fight very hard, to defend my presence in your heart. Love attack, love attack, hey, baby; are you aware of the fact, love attack, love attack will put you smack flat on your back? Love attack, love attack, be prepared for my love attacks.

Love Blinds the Mind

Albert Humphries

Love blinds the mind, I ain't lying. Baby, stop being so doggone kind, you are actually blowing my mind. I ain't lying, love blinds the mind, love blinds the mind. You treated me so divine, you offered your love, I didn't decline. Last night you said that you are mine, now I'm in a sensual state of mind, which is difficult for me to define. I ain't lying, love blinds the mind. Baby, stop being so doggone kind, you are actually blowing my mind. I ain't lying, love blinds the mind, love blinds the mind. I don't know a nickel from a dime, I have lost track of the time. And on the job, I'm falling behind, I can feel it in my spine, that I'm losing my mind. I ain't lying, love blinds the mind. Baby, stop being so doggone kind, you are actually blowing my mind. I ain't lying, love blinds the mind, love blinds the mind. Your burning affection makes me whine, I go bananas when our love is combined. But this is the way our affair is designed. Baby, I let you put me into a bind, but your sweet love I just couldn't decline, I had to find. I ain't lying, love blinds the mind. Baby, stop being so doggone kind, you are actually blowing my mind. I ain't lying, love blinds the mind, love blinds the mind.

Love-e-o

Albert Humphries

Hey, baby, for the time being forget your phone, radio, stereo, audio and video. Tune in on me, your one and only love-e-o. Yes, I'm right here on the scene, I'm your live audio/video love machine. I'm a brand-new flashy flesh game, come in and let me drive you insane. Oh, yeah, I'm a game of thrills and chills and possess the will to fulfill. Your love-e-o has audio, enabling you to hear the sound of passion, your love-e-o has video, enabling you to see the action. Yes, love-e-o is my trademark and brand name, loving is the description of my games. I play for kicks and I play only with chicks. So, if you like videos, you will love me, your one and only, love-e-o.

Love Came Pouring Out

Albert Humphries

Last year when her birthday was near, she made it known, she made it clear, her gift was all she whined and gabbed about; around that time her love came pouring out. She practiced her tactics of love play and kept it up until her birthday, and then her love really came pouring out. Last week when her girlfriend was here, she made it known, she made it clear, that I'm her main man, she left no doubts, around that time her love came pouring out. Suddenly she was all sugar and spice, pampering me and being extremely nice, and then her love came pouring out. Last night she came whispering in my ear, she made it known, she made it clear, that she is no longer a little Girl Scout, around that time her love came pouring out. She claimed she loved me with all her heart and to prove it, let her play the part and then her love really came pouring out.

Love Is a Necessity

Albert Humphries

Like a car must have gas for it to go, I must have your love,
I need it so. I'm depending on you to provide the love I des-
perately need to survive. Love is a necessity; everybody desires it, more or less. Love is a necessity, the main ingredient
for happiness. Love is a necessity, I got to have it, I got to
have it. For some strange reason, I feel insecure. Baby, do
you love me? Are you for sure? I'm confused and upset most
of the time, without love, there's no peace of mind. Love is a
necessity; everybody desires it, more or less. Love is a necessity, the main ingredient for happiness. Love is a necessity, I
got to have it, I got to have it. Don't let your so-called friends
fool you, they need love just like you do. I demand your love
every single day, so don't you dare take it away. Love is a necessity, everybody desires it, more or less. Love is a necessity,
the main ingredient for happiness. Love is a necessity.

Love Is Under Investigation

Albert Humphries

The way my life is coming along, very soon I'll be alone. I never figured I knew enough to be sly, but at least enough to get me by. Is it me, my mate or just another mistake, I got to find out before it's too late. Love is under investigation, when all the evidence is in, then the proceedings can begin. Love is under investigation. I need a superlative and super-permanent grip, in order to maintain a steady relationship. Where do I begin? Where do I look? In someone's "survey of love" book? I need a lead; do I plant a few seeds? And wait for them to grow, then proceed? I'm going to explore every avenue, until I come up with the perfect clue. Love is under investigation. What are the real hardcore facts, it's like looking for a needle in a haystack. Love is under investigation. Yes, my personal feelings are definitely included, along with the pure facts, I have concluded, that love has many, many, many different definitions, and it depends on each person's current condition. Because love affects different people in different ways, as different as the passing days. Love is an ongoing learning process; the flow of new information will never rest. Therefore, love is now and always will be under investigation.

Love It Up

Albert Humphries

Baby, let's love it up, let's love it up, let's love it up. Why sit around in sorrow, love today, don't wait for tomorrow. You live only once in this life, so love it up and do it right. Come on, let go, have a heart, I'm willing and able to do my part. Let's love it up, let's love it up; once the love torch is lit, the burning passion won't let you quit. Sizzle, baby, sizzle; burn, baby, burn; loving it up is easy to learn. Love it up, love it up, love it up; loving it up is living it up. It's as simple as drinking from a cup. You're doing it like I knew you would, you never knew the feeling was so good. Love it up, love it up, love it up; I'm convinced we'll love it up forever, loving it up with you is pretty darn clever. We will love it up until the end of time, loving it up won't cost you a dime. So, we will keep on living it up, we will keep on loving it up. We will love it up, love it up, love it up.

My Love Alarm

Albert Humphries

My love alarm, my love alarm, it works like a charm. My love alarm, my love alarm, it's programmed to warn. Baby, you are extraordinarily appealing. I have discovered a brand-new feeling. I'm glad that I won't be alone when this new sensation is turned on. Baby, once you apply your charm, you will activate my love alarm. My love alarm, my love alarm, it works like a charm. My love alarm, my love alarm, it's programmed to warn. Baby, I don't need any more hints, I know what my love alarm meant. I'm always ready to put out your fire, I will fulfill my greatest desire. I can't wait to experience the thrills, let's get started with the love drills. My love alarm, my love alarm, it works like a charm. My love alarm, my love alarm, it's programmed to warn. Baby, you will release your sugar and spice, you will make the love drill nice. Honey, never forget what you are supposed to do, whenever the love wave hits you. Don't hesitate to fall into my arms, you will automatically activate the alarm. My love alarm, my love alarm, it works like a charm. My love alarm, my love alarm, it's programmed to warn.

Practice Love

Albert Humphries

In the world of love, malpractice is a laughing matter, you don't get worse, only better. Practicing love makes perfect love, so practice it; practice, practice, practice. Doctors practice medicine, soldiers practice war, I practice love and it's the best so far. Lawyers practice law, criminals practice crime, I practice love, practically all the time. Oh, yes, I do practice what I preach and you are the one I wish to teach. If you want to learn new love tactics, you must put your sweet self into practice. Are you striving for that maximum height? Well, I'm conducting a practice session tonight. I told my boss no overtime for me, I'm going home, that's where I'll be. So, if you feel you are not up to par, come on over, I don't live far. Practicing is the practical thing to do and I'm really ready to practice with you. Practice love makes perfect love. So, practice it; practice, practice, practice.

That Good Ole Sweet Love

Albert Humphries

We were sitting in the backyard swing, suddenly she started to sing. I placed on her face a soft and tender kiss, she sang about love and it went like this. What can more or less produce tears of happiness and at the same time can turn a situation completely around, from one extreme to the other, creating hatred between one another? What is this force? The answer, of course, is good ole sweet love. That good ole sweet love. What can compel one to compete? What can make life virtually complete? What can stimulate the heart in countless ways? Many different sensations for many different days. What can make one mad, glad or sad? What is it that everybody wishes they had? What is this force? The answer, of course, is good ole sweet love. That good ole sweet love.

The Impulse of Love

Albert Humphries

I can feel a strong urge inside of me itching for your love to come and set it free. I'm sorry if I'm coming on too strong, I just don't want to wait too long. I move on impulse, can't you see? So, you better watch out for me. You better watch out for me. I move on impulse. The impulse of love, the impulse of love. I hope you can stand the sensation; my body transmits hot vibrations. Do you think you can handle this stimulating force? I'll make you come alive, with mighty love, of course. I move on impulse, can't you see? So, you better watch out for me. You better watch out for me; I move on impulse. The impulse of love, the impulse of love. Come on and enjoy some love with me, just you and I, the way it should be. I see no need for delay, you know you are the reason I act this way. I move on impulse, can't you see? So, you better watch out for me. You better watch out for me; I move on impulse. The impulse of love, the impulse of love.

The Other Lover

Albert Humphries

Yes, I admit at first, I thought I was the only guy, I was convinced, I had someone not even a millionaire could buy. Then gradually she started acting peculiar and very strange, I mean her attitude made a tremendous and stupendous change. Quite naturally, I immediately checked it out, I confronted her hoping to eradicate all doubts. She explained, she didn't notice anything that wasn't ordinary, even though her actions were to the contrary. So, early one night, when she decided not to stay, I followed her and it was only three blocks away. I saw her approach him, I stood in disbelief, there he was, a middle-aged guy waiting patiently. As the streetlight beamed down on her smiling face, they slowly and affectionately embraced. I should have snatched and slapped her and clobbered him, I was so hurt and angry, I could have killed them. Instead of losing control and throwing blows, I watched them ease on down the narrow road. My teary and weary eyes had seen the true light, I continued watching as they faded into the darkness of the night. I approached her the very next day; she was petrified and didn't have too much to say. I asked her to confess and just tell me the plain truth, she responded with a stupid off-the-wall excuse. She said he was an old friend, of an old friend, and he was out looking for the other friend and ran into a dead end. And he needed her to help with the directions, I yelled stop! Stop! Let me make a few corrections. You're a big fat liar, he's your other lover and I'm a fool to think there wasn't another. Okay, honey, which one will it be, him or me? Well, let me help you make up your mind; goodbye, good luck and thanks for the happy times.

This Lonely Lovely Letter

Albert Humphries

These business trips are killing me, with you is where I prefer to be. I'm writing under candlelight, a hurricane struck here last night. I tried to call a hundred times. But the storm knocked out the phone lines. I'm writing you this lonely lovely letter, to let you know I'm safe and sound, just love sick that you are not around. This lonely lovely letter, is definitely making me feel better. Even though we are far apart, your sweet love lingers in my heart. If you feel the same as I do, then you must be missing me too. So why don't you follow my tracks, make me happy by writing me back? I'm writing you this lonely lovely letter, to let you know I'm missing you, to let you know I'm feeling blue. This lonely lovely letter, is definitely making me feel better. I've been away from you much too long, before you know it, I'll be home. This confession sealed with a kiss, is written for the one I truly miss. This lonely lovely letter, is definitely making me feel better.

Total Love

Albert Humphries

What did you say? You want me to stay? Okay, but you must love me in the conventional way. Love is more than dreaming and talking about it, it's sharing your body, your heart and your wits. I need your total love, don't shortchange and hold back on me. One hundred percent is what it's got to be. I need your total love. Love is something we all tend to pretend. Yes, even you do it every now and then, but this time please lead me in the right direction, I want more than a sample of your affection. I need your total love. Why not release your innermost emotions, which will neutralize any negative notions? I need your total love. Let's move on to higher heights, if we're going to do it, let's do it right. Love me properly, don't come half-stepping, complete honesty is all I'm expecting. I need your total love. So sweetheart, get smart and love me with all your heart. I need your total love.

Why Don't You Love Me?

Albert Humphries

It's not a question of morality, you claimed you like my personality. You said I'm a perfect gentleman in every way and this is the way you wanted me to stay. Without any persuasion on my part, you also said, you didn't mind being my sweetheart. But, you never, never mentioned love. Why don't you? I love you, but you don't love me. Why don't you love me? You stated definitely and repeatedly, that you cherish and honor my family. Your admirations are astounding, you admire me and you admire my surroundings. Admiring me is okay, alright, swell, but is it possible to love me just as well? You see, you never, never mentioned love. Why don't you? I love you, but you don't love me. Why don't you love me? Creating fun in bed, it seems I pass the test, you're consistently telling me that I'm the best. Now, tell me the truth; is this the bottom line, you love me for my sex and not for my mind? I'm still unable to find the key, I've been searching from A to Z. You see, you never, never mentioned love. Why don't you? I love you, but you don't love me. Why don't you love me?